Kentucky Troll

For Dennis Havill, my favorite troll.
—JH

For Emily Bush
and in memory of Sam Bush.
—BD

Library of Congress Cataloging in Publication Data
Havill, Juanita. Kentucky troll / by Juanita Havill: illustrated by Bert Dodson.
p.   cm.   Summary: A Swedish troll emigrates to Kentucky and tries to live there in disguise among the
humans, using his magic powder to make butter and luring a pretty girl to his cabin.   ISBN 0-688-10457-6.
—ISBN 0-688-10458-4 (lib. bdg.) [1. Fairy tales. 2. Trolls—Fiction. 3. Kentucky—Fiction.] I. Dodson,
Bert, ill. II. Title. PZ8.H287Ke   1992   [E]—dc20   90-27850 CIP AC

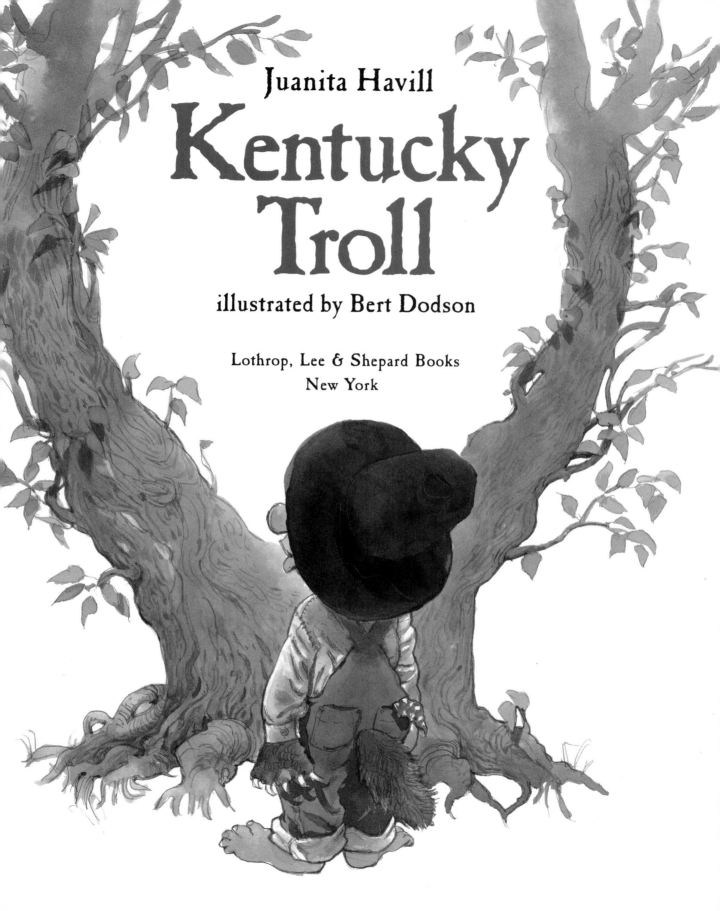

Juanita Havill

Kentucky Troll

illustrated by Bert Dodson

Lothrop, Lee & Shepard Books
New York

LONG AGO, the villages in Sweden became so crowded that people began to move into the woods.

Old Troll grumbled when he saw them come. "Trolls and people can't live together," he said.

"Why is that?" asked his son, Young Troll.

But Old Troll didn't explain. He just packed up his goods and moved his family north to the mountains— all except for Young Troll, that is, who would not go. For all his trollish ways, Young Troll was curious about people.

People were always doing something. Young Troll watched them clear the land, scratch the rocky earth, plant their fields, and harvest. He heard them complain about their spindly crops. He listened to them talk of a wonderful new land where the harvest never failed and streams flowed knee-deep with fish. And when some of them made plans to sail there, Young Troll decided to go, too. He took his sack of troll powder and stowed away in a barrel on a ship bound for America.

Midvoyage, the kitchen boy pried open Young Troll's barrel. Instead of bacon, he saw a hairy paw, a shaggy head, and the hint of a furry tail.

"A troll! Come quick!" shouted the boy. Soon a crowd gathered around. Shouting and pointing their fingers at Young Troll, they tossed the barrel into the ocean.

Luckily for Young Troll, it was a sturdy barrel. Though he drifted for days, alone and miserable, when at last he washed ashore, he was not much the worse for it. He tucked his tail into his trousers, thrust his paw into his pocket, and told the people who found him that he had been shipwrecked. Although his wrinkled skin and slitted green eyes seemed strange to them, the people helped him. They'd never heard of trolls—they didn't come from Sweden.

A farmer persuaded Young Troll to ride with him to Kentucky. "It'll be right nice to have some company on the journey," he said. "Name's Hiram. What do you call yourself?"

Young Troll frowned and thought. He didn't call himself anything. His family had called him Young Troll. "Young—" he started to say, but the farmer interrupted.

"John? Did you say John? Now, that's a good name."

Young Troll nodded. John was as good a people name as any.

"I expect you'll settle down in Kentucky and look for

a wife," said the farmer. "You'll have to build a house first. And you'll need some cows for your farm. Your wife will be wanting milk and butter. 'Course, you'll need some coins about you. It helps to have some money to win a wife." The farmer stared at Young Troll for a moment. "'Specially if you're not real handsome to look at."

By the time they reached Kentucky, Young Troll's thoughts were tossing about in his mind like barrels on a stormy sea. Wife, house, butter, money. People thoughts. Young Troll had never had people thoughts before.

Kentucky was a green and beautiful land with woods and hills and waterfalls, good caves to live in, and plenty of squirrels and rabbits to eat. Young Troll lived much as he had in Sweden, spending part of each day near the town, watching the people.

He watched them milk their cows and churn their butter and chop wood and wash and hang their laundry. He watched some of them go into the general store carrying buckets of butter and come out again with coins jingling in their pockets. He watched others give coins to the man behind the counter and come out with butter or bags of flour and sugar. And when he watched the smoke curl up from the chimneys of people's cabins, he felt a great longing to live like a person instead of a troll.

Young Troll began to build a cabin, but he quickly grew tired of chopping and notching the logs, so he sprinkled a pinch of troll powder on the wood to make the work go faster. Soon he had a comfortable, cozy cabin and, in no time, a barn as well.

Now he needed a cow. With a cow he could get the little round coins the farmer had said he needed for a wife.

After dark Young Troll went from farm to farm until he found a cow he liked. He led her back to his barn.

In the morning, he sprinkled troll powder on his new cow. Then he began to milk her. As long as he milked, the milk kept flowing.

Young Troll poured some milk in the churn and sprinkled on a pinch of troll powder. The churn wriggled and turned and bounced up and down until a fine lump of butter formed.

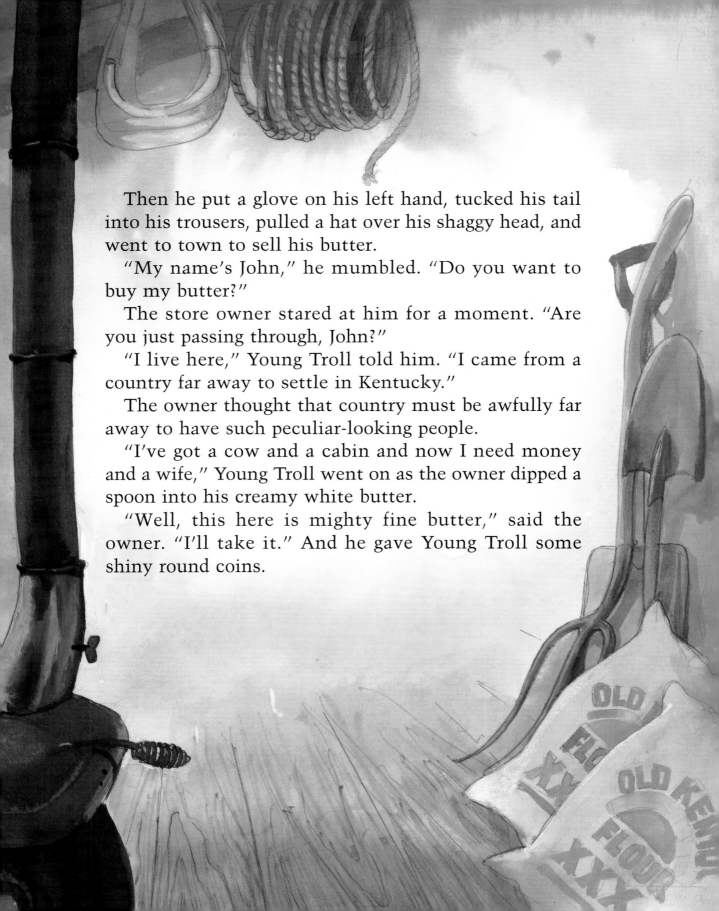

Then he put a glove on his left hand, tucked his tail into his trousers, pulled a hat over his shaggy head, and went to town to sell his butter.

"My name's John," he mumbled. "Do you want to buy my butter?"

The store owner stared at him for a moment. "Are you just passing through, John?"

"I live here," Young Troll told him. "I came from a country far away to settle in Kentucky."

The owner thought that country must be awfully far away to have such peculiar-looking people.

"I've got a cow and a cabin and now I need money and a wife," Young Troll went on as the owner dipped a spoon into his creamy white butter.

"Well, this here is mighty fine butter," said the owner. "I'll take it." And he gave Young Troll some shiny round coins.

Young Troll was pleased. Each week he brought butter to the store, and each week the owner gave him coins.

"Can you bring more butter?" the owner asked. "There ain't no better butter in town. Folks all ask for it, even them that makes their own. If you need some help, my Becky can milk your cow in the mornings. She's a good worker."

Becky was a strong young woman with freckles and hair the color of marigolds. Although he didn't need help, Young Troll figured that she would be good company.

Becky thought the stranger named John was odd. She didn't want to go, but her father was eager to find out the secret of John's butter, and so she went.

On their way to his cabin, Young Troll thought he should behave the way people do and say something to Becky, but he couldn't think what. "You don't have to be scared of trolls up here," he finally blurted out.

"I ain't skeered of trolls," said Becky. "What're trolls?"

"Trolls," Young Troll told her, "are not people. They live in the hills and the woods. Sometimes they're bigger than people and sometimes they're smaller. They have furry heads, wrinkled skin, and long tails. Their left hands look like bear paws. And they have magical ways."

"Oh, there ain't no such thing," said Becky, and she laughed.

Her laughter made Young Troll want to laugh, too. If she liked to hear about trolls, he would tell her more. After all, he knew all about them.

In the barn, Young Troll set a stool beside his cow. When Becky wasn't looking, he sprinkled troll powder on the cow. Then while Becky milked, he carried the buckets into his cabin.

Each morning Becky came to milk. "I ain't never seen so much milk," she kept saying, and Young Troll smiled from ear to ear with pride.

"I can churn too, if you like," said Becky, hoping to see how he made his butter.

"No need," snapped Young Troll.

Becky was surprised. Although his manner was always gruff, he had never before been sharp with her.

Each morning when they finished, Young Troll told Becky more about trolls. He liked to hear her laugh. "Trolls use magic powder to make their work easier," he would say. "They live for one hundred years."

And Becky always did laugh. "There ain't no such thing as trolls," she said. Then she took the marvelous butter to her father. The next morning she brought back coins.

Young Troll spread the coins all over the floor of his cabin. Some he hung from the rafters of the barn—he liked to see them shining in the sun. Surely he would soon have enough money to win himself a wife.

"You ought to put your money away," Becky told him when she saw the coins hanging in the barn. "Somebody'll see it and steal it from you."

"Steal?" said Young Troll. He didn't know what "steal" meant. If a thing was there, you took it, that was all. Like the cow.

"These coins are for my wife," said Young Troll. He looked at her with his squinty eyes as soft as he could make them. Becky turned to the cow and started milking as fast as she could.

Young Troll watched her fill two buckets, all the while thinking what a fine wife she would be. Then he carried the buckets into his cabin and poured them into the churn. He was so caught up in his plans for Becky that he never noticed she was following him.

Young Troll pulled out his sack of troll powder. He dipped his fingers in for a pinch, but just as he did, he looked up. There at the window stood Becky, her eyes wide. Young Troll was so surprised that he dropped his whole sack of powder into the churn.

The churn started shaking and pumping and gurgling and rattling like a thing gone wild. Young Troll was furious. Not only had he been discovered, he had lost all his troll powder.

He ripped off his hat and threw it on the floor—his shaggy hair sprang out. He shook his fist and his glove fell off—there was his bear paw. In a rage, he jumped on his hat and glove, up and down as hard as he could. His tail slipped out and dragged on the floor.

Becky turned white and caught her breath. "Troll! Troll!" she screamed. "You're a troll!" And she ran back to town as fast as she could.

Becky told everyone that the butter maker was really a troll. "What is a troll?" they all asked, and Becky tried to explain.

"Trolls are strange, ugly creatures that live to be a hundred. They have bear paws and tails like beasts. They're magical, too, and they use troll powder."

"There ain't no such thing as trolls," the people said.

Becky led them back to the cabin so they could see for themselves, but no one was there. The churn was still turning out butter—it poured down the sides and onto the floor—and the people agreed that something very strange had happened. But Young Troll was gone, and so were his shiny coins. The cow was in the barn, and the people led her back to her owner. They left the cabin as it was.

Young Troll went back to his cave. He tossed the coins on the cave floor. "People and trolls can't live together," he grumbled, "even in this new land."

But often he crept back to his cabin and hid in the woods to watch for Becky, who came each day to collect the creamy white butter from the magic churn. How peculiar people are, he thought. And what a relief not to have to act like them!

For the rest of his days, Young Troll lived the life of a troll in the wild, green land of Kentucky...but he never gave up his people-watching ways.